Toad Catchers' Creek

Written By
Brian Weiner

Illustrated By
Martin Cannon

Edited By
Claudia Weintraub
Robin Frederick

Digitally Remastered By
Sahak Ekshian

A Labor of Love By
The Illusion Factory
Woodland Hills, CA
www.IllusionFactoryKids.com

Toad Catchers' Creek
Merchandise and Apparel

Designed By Karen Toal Anderson

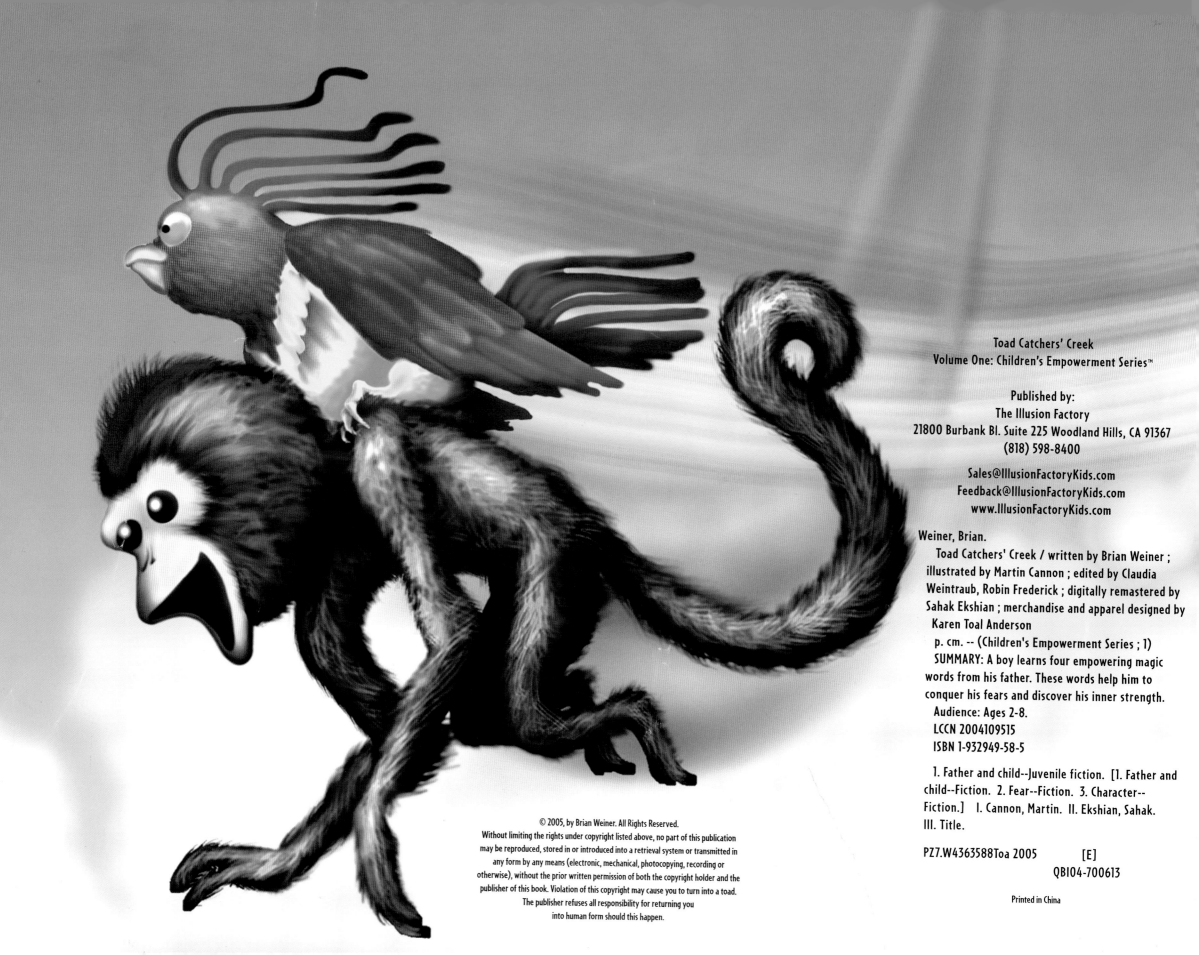

Toad Catchers' Creek
Volume One: Children's Empowerment Series™

Published by:
The Illusion Factory
21800 Burbank Bl. Suite 225 Woodland Hills, CA 91367
(818) 598-8400

Sales@IllusionFactoryKids.com
Feedback@IllusionFactoryKids.com
www.IllusionFactoryKids.com

Weiner, Brian.
   Toad Catchers' Creek / written by Brian Weiner ;
illustrated by Martin Cannon ; edited by Claudia
Weintraub, Robin Frederick ; digitally remastered by
Sahak Ekshian ; merchandise and apparel designed by
Karen Toal Anderson
   p. cm. -- (Children's Empowerment Series ; 1)
   SUMMARY: A boy learns four empowering magic
words from his father. These words help him to
conquer his fears and discover his inner strength.
   Audience: Ages 2-8.
   LCCN 2004109515
   ISBN 1-932949-58-5

   1. Father and child--Juvenile fiction. [1. Father and
child--Fiction. 2. Fear--Fiction. 3. Character--
Fiction.] I. Cannon, Martin. II. Ekshian, Sahak.
III. Title.

PZ7.W4363588Toa 2005   [E]
QBI04-700613

Printed in China

Don't tell me it is impossible... until after I have already done it!

Setting out to accomplish any new task, large or small, is an endeavor that requires two parts courage and four parts determination. Some tasks are so daunting that we are quick to dismiss our real potentials. It is easier to concede than it is to face our fears of failure. In many cases, we opt to quit without having tried.

Toad Catchers' Creek is a true story and the magic is real. It is warmly retold here as the debut volume of the Children's Empowerment Series™, which is written to train young minds to confront and thereby eventually overcome their fears. In the formative years, we are imprinted with a core of what makes us our special selves. By creating the Children's Empowerment Series, I am trying through my own grassroots effort to make a difference in this world by sharing some of what I have learned along my journey on Planet Earth.

I believe that a company's greatest resource is its people. At The Illusion Factory™, I encourage my employees to grow in as many ways as their passions will lead them. In this spirit, The Illusion Factory has formed the I CAN DO IT CLUB to foster the hopes and dreams of as many open minds as we can attract. Our website: www.IllusionFactoryKids.com is dedicated to bringing opportunities, information, education and inspiration to aspiring minds (both young and old). The plan is simple...teach young children (and perhaps even their parents as well) to be bold and to go out into the world with a mindset that is geared to succeed. Then, we network all of them together through a single information portal in cyberspace and allow the magic of interconnectivity to work at its own pace. At www.IllusionFactoryKids.com we provide catalysts to help empower people to achieve their goals.

I do not presume that we have all of the answers, but by launching this venture, I will demonstrate in my own unique way that one person can make a difference...One person can help change the world. When this story actually took place, I was in a park with my son Christopher, who was four at the time. Once I had written the book, the energy that I invested in it doubled with the incredible talents of the illustrator, Martin Cannon. There is no doubt that my vision is greatly magnified in the presence of his arresting visual flair. From there, the number of contributing creative individuals has grown as this book continued to unfold. In the end, we will donate some of our proceeds to children's programs around the world, and I will have shown my own kids how we made a difference while at the same time spreading the good news...once empowered, YOU CAN DO ANYTHING!

I lost my father, Gerald Weiner, last year. He was the antithesis of the attorney jokes that have circulated throughout our society. He worked countless hours for free to ensure that lower income families had a chance for compassionate representation and he navigated many of them to safe harbor within our convoluted legal system. I dedicate this book to him, for the many loving lessons he spent his time teaching me.

I miss you Dad.

This book would not have been possible without the love and support of my wonderful soul mate–Claudia, our four kids–Bec, Marc, Chris, Laura, our boxers–Zoey and Pokey, and the rest of our humble menagerie–Chico (bird), Bunny (you guessed it), Tayo (black stallion), Buster (pony), and our very furry alpacas–Lace, Miss Minnie, Jacqueline, Josephine, Rocky, Paris, Touchstone, Adrianna and King James. They may be seen at www.IllusionFactoryKids.com.

And finally, I owe a tremendous debt of gratitude to my mother, Marise (a.k.a. Henry Higgins!), for her love, support, friendship, and her perpetual artistic influence on my life. She never failed to correct my grammar...hopefully her unswerving efforts in this area are readily apparent in this book.

High on the opposite shore across Toad Catchers' Creek,
loomed the legendary monkey bars of Willow Haven Peak.
If you'd climbed them you'd know they were rigid and steep...
and once at the top, you'd then have to leap.
It took courage and will, determination and pride,
to learn what you were made of...who you really were inside.

But there he stood, with the whole creek in view.
The Toad Catchers stopped and watched him, he knew.
For everyone cared if he did it or failed, and if he
backed out now... he knew he'd be nailed.

Standing to the side, watching his young son's face...
Chris' dad stood still and stayed in his place while his son
stared out at the many rows of bars that stretched ever
outward... even further than Mars!

Chris reached out and grabbed one with all of his will...

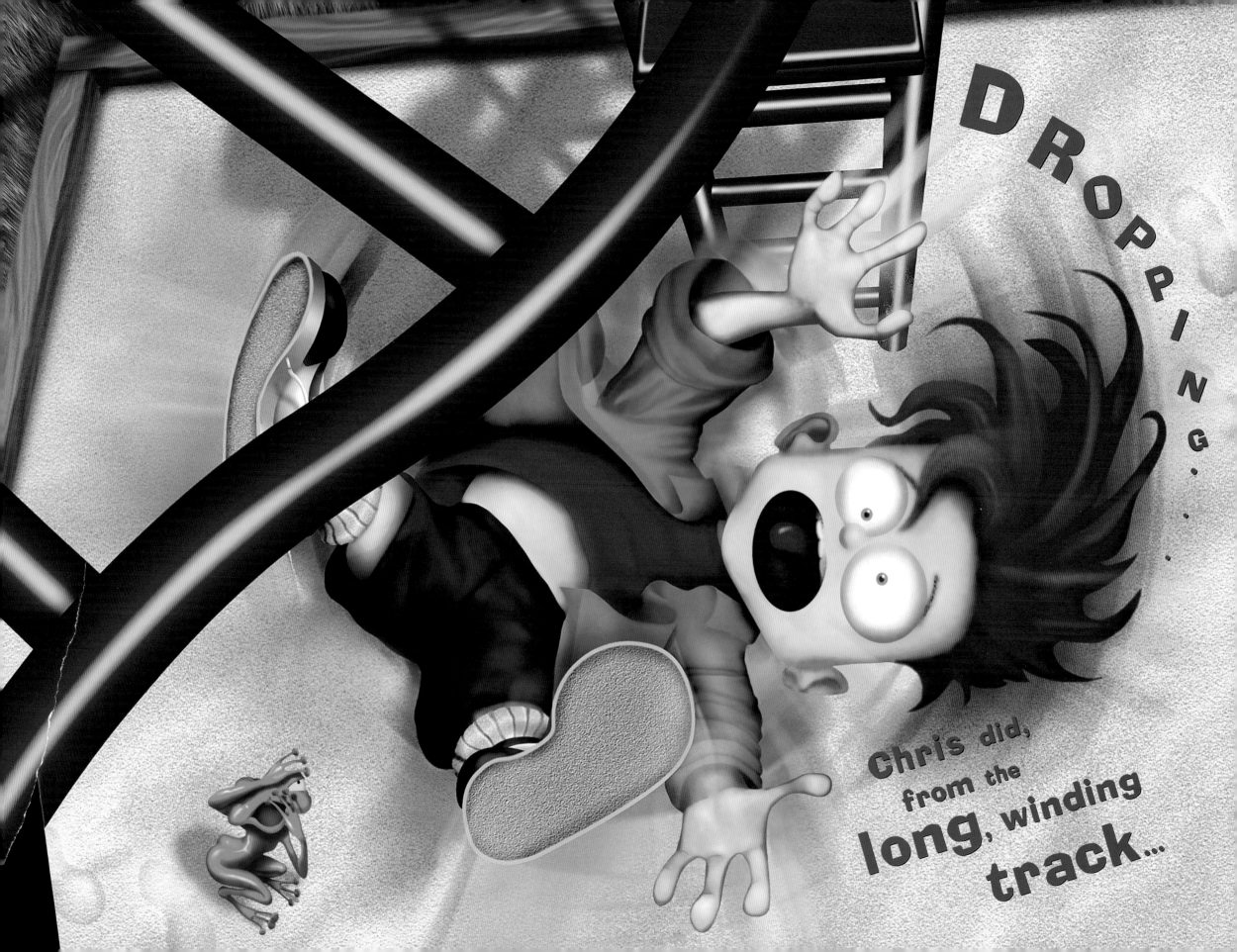

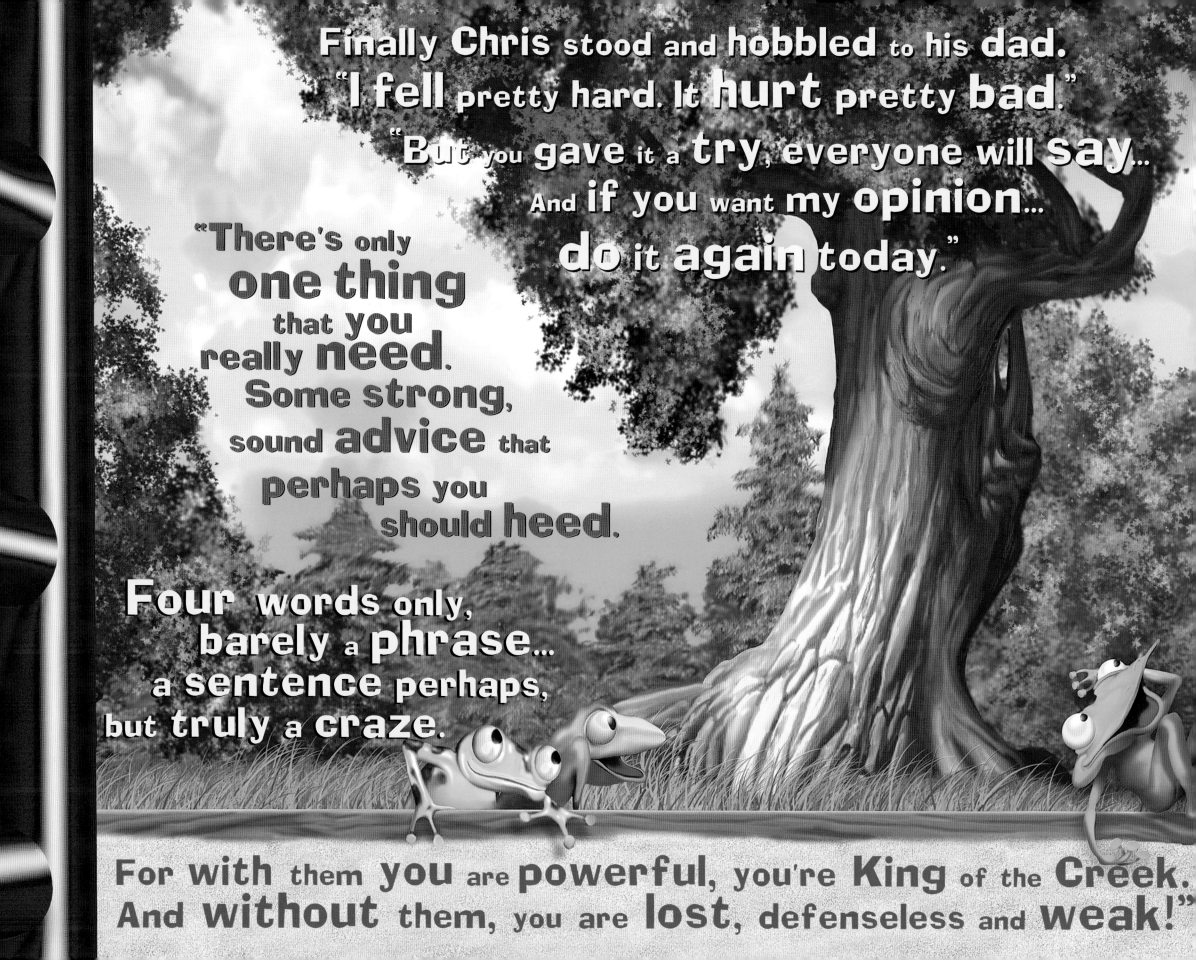

Finally Chris stood and hobbled to his dad. "I fell pretty hard. It hurt pretty bad." "But you gave it a try, everyone will say... And if you want my opinion... do it again today."

"There's only one thing that you really need. Some strong, sound advice that perhaps you should heed.

Four words only, barely a phrase... a sentence perhaps, but truly a craze.

For with them you are powerful, you're King of the Creek. And without them, you are lost, defenseless and weak!"

"I'll tell you a **story**
I **heard** long ago,
about a **little guy**
who lived **higher**
than the **crows**.
He was **young**
and quite **scared**,
defenseless and **wary**.
And when he
considered **flying**,
he thought it **was scary**.

There **once** was
a **Macaw**, youngest
and **smallest** of three...
who **lived**
far **atop**
a **towering**
tree."

Screech was ever so **happy** high **up** in his **nest** where everything was **easy**, so he **never** had to give his **best**. **Until** one **day** his brothers stretched their **wings** and **flew**...

Screech peered over the **edge** and turned incredibly **blue**.

He shook and he swayed, holding tight as he could...
but in his heart, he knew that he should
give it a try and give it his best.
This was his time... Was he up for the test?

He looked with
a frown at the water
pounding below,
then shook his head firmly
and chose not to go.
"I can't do it Tracker...
not NOW and not ever.
Mom keeps asking me 'When?'
and I always say never!"

His **mother** flew over, tucked Screech under her **wing**, looked him in the **eye** and told him **one** thing. "The four **magic** words that you need to hear...

...will **help** you, my son, to overcome your fear. It's okay to be **scared**, your **wings** will **not** rust... but these words give you **magic** to hold and to **trust**.

They're **simple** I **know**, but the **power** is **real**! Once you've **mastered** them, **just watch** how you feel!"

Screech opened his eyes with great delight... Hoping his mom's magic would help him with flight! "What are they, mom?" he asked with grand spirit. "They're simple," she said...

"I CAN DO IT."

Screech looked around, hoping for the best, but when he peeked down below, he failed the test. Because to say the words was one thing, but to believe them another.

Screech still did not believe he could fly like his brother.

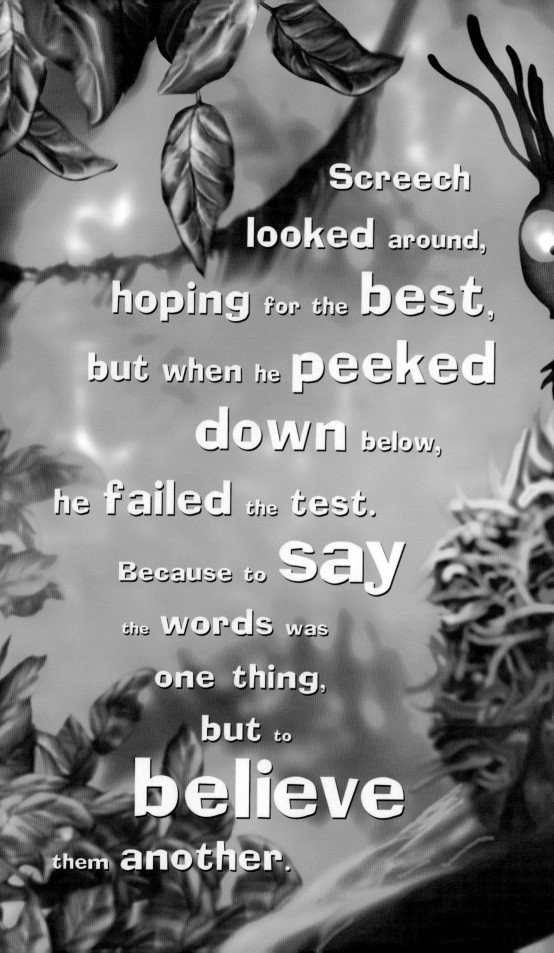

Till one day
he was moping...
all alone in the tree,
when he heard
a loud wail, and whom
did he see?

One tree over, his friend Tracker was falling!
And guess whose name Tracker was calling?
"Help me Screech!"
He made a loud sound.
"Please catch me quickly before I hit the ground!"

"I CAN DO IT!" Screech yelled, as he plunged out of the nest, while spreading his wings, and trying his best. For his friend was in danger, that's all Screech knew. It was up to him, or Tracker was through!

Dodging branches and sticks, Screech swooped down from the tree. His falling buddy was all he could see.

Until **finally** he had **him**, **clenched** in his **wings** and he **knew** he had **saved** him from **terrible things!**

He stood up
and climbed
the tall,
rigid stairs...
And on the back
of his neck,
he could feel
all of his
hairs.

Again he stood, standing straight and true and looked out at his friends and wondered who had ever used these words before him that day. And if asked if they worked, what would THEY say?

He looked down at his dad, who nodded and smiled, watching a new sense of bravery surge in his child. Chris muttered the words, his dad said, "LOUDER!" Then Chris screamed them. Dad couldn't have been prouder.

Chris swooped outward...his wings stretched towards the sky...This was his chance... he knew he must try.

As Chris **blazed** his way, the Toad Catchers **stopped** to **see**...

the newest **bird** on the **playground...**
soar from his **tree!**

Chris' dad ran around, **hugging** his son with **pride.** "I knew you could **do it** Chris, way deep **inside."**

Someday you'll have a child with whom you shall speak
and you'll know to tell them of Toad Catchers' Creek...
The words you have learned are famous and true
and when that little face is looking up at you...
You will share with them the lesson of today.
And with much love and warmth,
it will be your pleasure to say...
That this was the magic you got from your dad...
and when you see your child get it...
you will certainly be glad.